The TERRIBLE PLOP

Ursula Dubosarsky

Pictures by Andrew Joyner

For my parents, with love
Ursula

For Beck, William and Charlotte
Andrew

EGMONT
We bring stories to life

First published by
Penguin Group (Australia) 2009

First published in the UK by
Egmont UK Limited 2010

Text copyright © Ursula Dubosarsky 2009
Illustrations copyright © Andrew Joyner 2009

The moral rights of the author and illustrator
have been asserted

ISBN: 978 1 4052 5136 5 (hb)
ISBN: 978 1 4052 5137 2 (pb)

10 9 8 7 6 5 4 3 2 1

A CIP catalogue record for this title
is available from The British Library

Printed and bound in Singapore

This story was inspired by a folktale from Tibet.

Six little rabbits
down by the lake,
munching on carrots
and chocolate cake.

Next to the lake
in a tree up high,
a round red apple
swings in the sky.

Soft is the wind
and the tree bends low.
The round red apple
is all aglow.

Suddenly comes
a terrible

PLOP!

Up jump the rabbits –
hop hop hop!

They shout to each other,
'Run! Don't stop!
We must get away
from the Terrible PLOP!'

'Wait, little rabbits,'
calls the fox as they pass.
'Where are you hopping to
so very fast?'

But the rabbits cry back,
'We cannot stop!
We must get away
from the Terrible PLOP!'

The Terrible PLOP?
thinks the fox in fear,
Maybe I'd better
get out of here!

'Goodbye, friend monkey,
I cannot stop –
I must get away
from the Terrible PLOP!'

He runs with the rabbits,
the monkey and the cat,

the pig and the elephant,

the tiger and the bat.

Soon all of the animals,
one by one,
out of the forest
they come at a run.

Out comes the leopard!
Out comes the goose!
Out comes the antelope!
Out comes the moose!

They do not stay.
They do not stop.
They run run run
from the Terrible PLOP.

At last they come
to the big brown bear,
sunning himself
in a folding chair.

'What's this?' says the big brown bear
with a frown.
'Where are you running to?
Stop! Slow down!'

'No, no, brown bear,
we cannot stop.
We must get away
from the Terrible PLOP!'

'The Terrible PLOP?
What do I care,
about a silly old PLOP?'
yawns the big brown bear.

'Oh no, brown bear,' they cry.
'You're wrong!
The PLOP is fierce!
The PLOP is strong!
It's coming to get us,
It's coming, you'll see!'

'WHAT?'
growls the brown bear,
'Stronger than

ME?'

And he grabs with his paw
at the one coming last –
the littlest rabbit
who's not very fast.

The littlest rabbit
with the littlest hop,
but the greatest fear
of the Terrible PLOP.

'Now little rabbit,
you show me where
is the place of the PLOP,'
snarls the big brown bear.

'Oh please big bear,
don't make me go!
I'm very afraid
of the PLOP, you know!'

But the bear roars back.
'You show me where

OR I'LL EAT YOU UP!'

says the big brown bear.

Poor little rabbit.
Blink blink blink.
Poor little rabbit.
Think think think.

'I'm afraid of the PLOP.
I'm afraid of the bear.
But the bear is here
and the PLOP is there!'

Brave little rabbit,
hop hop hop.
Back to the lake
and the Terrible PLOP.

Big brown bear
slowly comes to a stop.
'So where,' says the bear,
'is this Terrible PLOP?'

The sun is soft,
the water is still.
An evening wind
rolls down from the hill.

Tall and dark
stands the big brown bear.
Dark and strong
with his nose in the air.

Next to the lake
in a tree up high,
a round red apple
swings in the sky.

Suddenly comes
a terrible

PLOP!

But this time the rabbit
does not hop.

The wind rolls down
from the top of the hill,
but this time the littlest rabbit
sits still.

And turns to speak
to the big brown bear.
But the big brown bear . . .

The rabbit calls out
to the big brown bear,
'Where are you going to
bear, O where?'

The bear cries back . . .

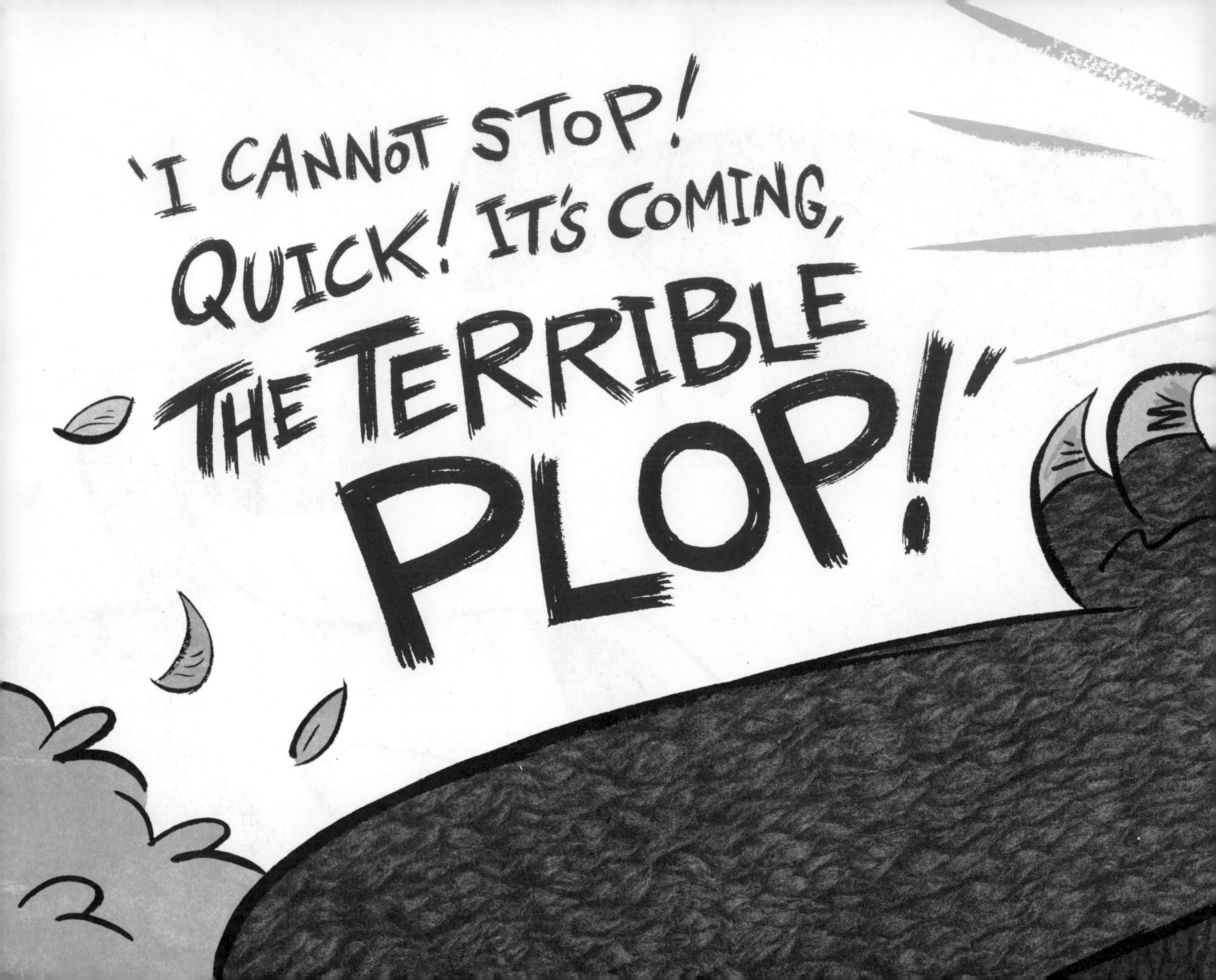
'I CANNOT STOP!
QUICK! IT'S COMING,
THE TERRIBLE
PLOP!'

One little rabbit
down by the lake,
happily munching on
chocolate cake.

'All this running
should really stop . . .

Who's afraid
of a silly old PLOP?'